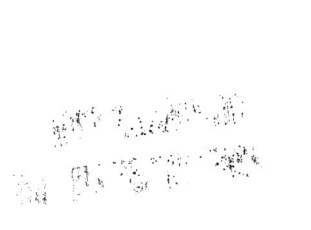

Handling
Asthma

by Alexis Burling

Content Consultant
Jennifer Shih, MD
Assistant Professor
Department of Medicine and Pediatrics
Emory University

Handling
Health Challenges

Essential Library
An Imprint of Abdo Publishing
abdobooks.com

abdobooks.com

Published by Abdo Publishing, a division of ABDO, PO Box 398166, Minneapolis, Minnesota 55439. Copyright © 2022 by Abdo Consulting Group, Inc. International copyrights reserved in all countries. No part of this book may be reproduced in any form without written permission from the publisher. Essential Library™ is a trademark and logo of Abdo Publishing.

Printed in the United States of America, North Mankato, Minnesota.
052021
092021

THIS BOOK CONTAINS RECYCLED MATERIALS

Cover Photo: iStockphoto
Interior Photos: Shutterstock Images, 4, 11, 14, 16, 19, 28, 36–37, 40, 43, 72, 77, 84, 90, 98–99; Monkey Business Images/Shutterstock Images, 8; Elisa Manzati/Shutterstock Images, 22; Kristi Blokhin/Shutterstock Images, 27; Koldunova Anna/Shutterstock Images, 33; Ramon Espinosa/AP Images, 47; Everett Collection/Shutterstock Images, 50; New York Public Library/Science Source, 56; GustoImages/Science Source, 59; Richard Drew/AP Images, 61; Galina Barskaya/Shutterstock Images, 62; Lyndon Stratford/iStockphoto, 67; Everyonephoto Studio/Shutterstock Images, 70–71; Jasminko Ibrakovic/Shutterstock Images, 74; Red Line Editorial, 83; SDI Productions/iStockphoto, 86; Smith Collection/Gado/Archive Images/Getty Images, 94; Aqnus Febriyant/Shutterstock Images, 97

Editor: Arnold Ringstad
Series Designer: Megan Ellis

Library of Congress Control Number: 2020948020

Publisher's Cataloging-in-Publication Data

Names: Burling, Alexis, author.
Title: Handling asthma / by Alexis Burling
Description: Minneapolis, Minnesota : Abdo Publishing, 2022 | Series: Handling health challenges | Includes online resources and index.
Identifiers: ISBN 9781532194931 (lib. bdg.) | ISBN 9781098215248 (ebook)
Subjects: LCSH: Asthma--Juvenile literature. | Asthmatics--Juvenile literature. | Asthma--Diagnosis--Juvenile literature. | Asthma--Treatment--Juvenile literature. | Respiration--Juvenile literature. | Health--Juvenile literature.
Classification: DDC 616.2--dc23

Contents

Chapter One
A HURDLE TO A DREAM 4

Chapter Two
SYMPTOMS AND CAUSES 16

Chapter Three
GETTING A DIAGNOSIS 28

Chapter Four
DISEASE DEMOGRAPHICS 40

Chapter Five
THE HISTORY OF ASTHMA 50

Chapter Six
ASTHMA AND PHYSICAL HEALTH 62

Chapter Seven
ASTHMA AND MENTAL HEALTH 74

Chapter Eight
TREATMENT AND BEYOND 86

Essential Facts	100	Index	110
Glossary	102	About the Author	112
Additional Resources	104	About the Consultant	112
Source Notes	106		

Chapter
One

A Hurdle to a Dream

It was Saturday night, December 14, 2019, and Jayna couldn't have been more excited. The day she had long been waiting for had almost arrived. In just a few hours, the 2019 National Junior Olympic Cross Country Championships would begin. This time, she wouldn't be cheering her teammates on from the sidelines. She'd be participating in the event alongside more than 4,000 other kids and teens ages seven to 18. Her race, the 5K for 17- and 18-year-old girls, was scheduled to kick off at 2:20 p.m. on Saturday. Jayna was ready—and she was more determined than ever to bring home a medal.

Ever since she could remember, Jayna's dream was to make the US Olympic Track and Field team. Growing up, she read every book and article she could find about Olympic track stars such as Jackie

Some activities, including long-distance running, can be challenging for those with asthma.

Joyner-Kersee, Wilma Rudolph, Wyomia Tyus, and Florence Griffith-Joyner. In 2016, she and her family traveled to Eugene, Oregon, to watch the Olympic trials to see who would qualify for the US Olympic team. She screamed as loud as she could from the stands when her favorite sprinter, Allyson Felix, finished the 400-meter race in just 49.68 seconds, beating Phyllis Francis for the gold.

Jayna wanted to be just like Felix. But up until a year ago, she didn't think it was possible. Though she loved anything having to do with track and field, her ability to run long distances or even sprint was declining. In the months leading up to the 2018 National Junior Olympic Cross Country Championships, she constantly felt out of breath while warming

Famous Athletes with Asthma

Most sports require fitness and endurance. This type of sustained, rigorous activity can be especially difficult for people who have trouble breathing. But contrary to popular belief, it is not only possible for people with asthma to participate in sports; it is also possible that they'll succeed, especially if the proper treatment protocol is followed. The record books are packed with athletes who overcame asthma on their way to the top. Some include track-and-field athlete Jackie Joyner-Kersee, a four-time Olympian and three-time gold medalist, and British long-distance runner Paula Radcliffe, who held the women's record for the fastest marathon for 16 years.

up or exercising. Jayna wanted to compete in the event. But her condition had gotten so bad that her coach suggested she drop out of the race and go see a doctor immediately. She was devastated and assumed that becoming a track star was no longer possible.

Jayna's Diagnosis

Jayna had watched the 2018 National Junior Olympic Cross Country Championships from the bleachers. The following Monday, her parents took her to see her primary care physician, who gave Jayna a referral to an allergist, a doctor who specializes in treating conditions related to allergies, including asthma. Luckily, the doctor had an opening that afternoon.

> "It took me a while to accept that I was asthmatic. It took me a while to even start taking my medication properly, to do the things that the doctor was asking me to do. I just didn't want to believe that I was an asthmatic. But once I stopped living in denial, I got my asthma under control, and I realized that it is a disease that can be controlled."[1]
>
> —*Jackie Joyner-Kersee, track-and-field star*

Jayna felt nervous during the appointment with the allergist. But with her mother holding her hand and the allergist explaining every step she was about to take, Jayna began to feel more at ease. First, the doctor asked Jayna a series of questions about her medical history, her family background, her activities, her diet, and how much sleep she was getting each night.

An allergist might interview a patient as part of an asthma diagnosis.

What Is Spirometry?

Spirometry is the main test doctors use in people ages five and older to determine if they have asthma. Patients inhale deeply, then exhale forcefully into a machine called a spirometer. The spirometer records the amount of air the person breathes out and the rate at which the person exhales. The entire process takes less than 15 minutes. During the test, the doctor looks at two readings. One is forced vital capacity (FVC), or the amount of air the person expels after breathing in as deeply as possible. The second is forced expiratory volume (FEV), which shows how much air the person can force from his or her lungs in one second. If either of these readings is below normal, it may indicate the presence of asthma or other lung diseases.

Normal results for a spirometry test can differ from person to person. They are based on a person's age, gender, weight, and height. Results are considered normal if they reach at least 80 percent or more of the predicted value. This predicted value can also be determined using an online calculator provided by the Centers for Disease Control and Prevention (CDC).

The doctor collected blood for testing. Using a stethoscope, she listened to Jayna's breathing for any signs of wheezing or congestion. She examined Jayna's chest, nose, throat, and skin for signs of eczema or other allergies. Finally, she used a device called a spirometer to check Jayna's lungs and see how fast she could exhale air.

At the end of the appointment, the doctor diagnosed Jayna with asthma. Thankfully Jayna's case was mild, but the doctor warned her that it could get much worse if Jayna didn't take steps to combat the symptoms. She gave Jayna a detailed treatment plan called an asthma action plan. It included a prescription for a daily medication that would keep the asthma under control. She wrote a second prescription for a quick-relief inhaler, also known as a rescue inhaler, that could be used in the short term in case Jayna experienced an asthma attack.

By the time the appointment was over, Jayna was pretty shaken up, but she was also relieved. Sure, she had a health condition she would have to monitor. But now that she could put a name to it and had a proper path to treatment, she could move forward with her life—and get back to running again.

Going for the Gold

After her doctor appointment, Jayna spent the next year getting her health back on track. She remembered to take her medicine daily and only used her inhaler when she truly needed it. She went back to see her doctor a few times, making sure that her condition wasn't getting worse and that she was taking all the necessary precautions.

Jayna also made up her mind to improve her diet and overall health. She gave up junk food, aside from the occasional popcorn at the movies, ate

Eating nutritious food and living a healthy lifestyle can make it easier to manage asthma.

tons of fruits and vegetables, and avoided fast-food restaurants when possible. She drank plenty of water to stay hydrated and tried to get at least eight hours of sleep per night. To her parents' unending pleasure, she kept her room exceptionally clean and free of dust.

Living with asthma didn't mean Jayna had to give up exercising. In fact, her doctor told her she could use her rescue inhaler before a run if she felt she needed it. Jayna worked closely with her coach to come up with a training regimen that would keep her in shape and improve her stats without pushing her too hard and triggering an asthma attack.

By the time December rolled around, Jayna was more than ready for the race. Unlike the previous year, when she had watched from the bleachers, she felt capable and confident she could win. As she laced up her shoes and jogged over to the starting line, she reflected on how far she had come. Looking up at the stands, she saw her parents waving and screaming her name. When the buzzer sounded, she sprinted off down the track.

Jayna didn't win the gold that day. But she did take home a medal. Better yet, she beat her own best time and only had to use her inhaler once. While she still had a long way to go to even get close to qualifying for the US Olympic Track and Field team, that wasn't really the important point.

Combination Inhalers

There are many types of inhalers. Each is used for a different purpose. Some inhalers, called combination inhalers, contain two different drugs. Each of these active medications works to treat a patient's asthma differently. Most combination inhalers have a steroid that aims to decrease inflammation in the airways. The other drug, called a bronchodilator, relaxes the smooth muscle in the lungs and widens the airways. Working together, these medicines decrease asthma symptoms. If prescribed by a doctor, combination inhalers have been proven to be a successful treatment option for many people suffering from asthma. Examples of combination inhalers include Advair, Symbicort, Dulera, and Breo.

The fact that she could still race like the wind while having asthma was all that mattered to her.

Asthma in the World

Jayna is a fictional character, but her experiences represent the challenges that millions of people with asthma face each day. Asthma affects more than 300 million people around the world. It is the most common chronic disease among children worldwide.[2] According to 2018 data from the Centers for Disease Control and Prevention (CDC), more than 24 million people in the United States have asthma, including nearly six million children under the age of 18. That's about 7.7 percent of the adult population and 7.5 percent of children.[3] The disease affects people of all genders, ages, and ethnic backgrounds.

> "I don't think asthma affected my career—if anything it made me more determined to reach my potential. If you learn to manage your asthma and take the correct medication there's no reason you shouldn't be the best."[4]
>
> —*Paula Radcliffe, world-class marathon runner*

With today's treatments and a good knowledge of the disease, patients are able to handle life with asthma.

Living with asthma can affect all parts of daily life. It can impact schoolwork or office work, social relationships, family life, and even driving. Daily medication and frequent medical appointments can also be a financial strain. In the United States, asthma accounts for 9.8 million doctor's office visits, nearly 190,000 discharges from hospital inpatient care, and 1.8 million emergency room visits each year.[5]

Yet despite the seemingly grim outlook, it is possible to live a happy, healthy, and fulfilling life as an asthmatic—a person who has asthma—as long as the proper treatment protocol is followed. "Asthma is a chronic illness, meaning that it's never completely cured. Due to that, it's important that you try to be knowledgeable of the potential long-term consequences," says Joshua Davidson, a practicing physician and board-certified specialist in allergy, immunology, and pediatrics. "While asthma cannot be cured, it can be managed. There are steps you can take to control asthma symptoms and limit its long-term effects."[6]

Chapter *Two*

Symptoms and Causes

Asthma is a long-term medical condition. It affects each person differently. In order to understand what happens during an asthma attack, it's important to first think about how the respiratory system works under normal circumstances.

In a healthy individual, air enters the respiratory system through the nose and mouth. It then travels through the trachea, into the bronchial tubes, through smaller air passages called bronchioles, and finally into tiny air sacs in the lungs called alveoli. Oxygen in the inhaled air passes from the alveoli into the bloodstream through small blood vessels called capillaries. The capillaries then deliver this oxygen-rich blood to pulmonary veins, which lead to the left side of the heart. From the heart, the blood gets pumped throughout the rest of the body,

Breathing, one of the body's most vital functions, can be impaired by asthma.

> "Asthma is not a static disease. Your symptoms will wax and wane over time and be different from those of others."[1]
>
> —Dr. Pat Bass, an expert on asthma

providing the oxygen that the body's tissues need to function.

In a non-asthmatic person, the muscles around the bronchial tubes are relaxed. The airways remain open and unobstructed, allowing oxygen to easily reach the lungs. But in someone who suffers from asthma, the respiratory system behaves differently. During an asthma attack, the muscles around the bronchial tubes tighten. Airways in the lungs become inflamed and filled with mucus. This makes it difficult for air to freely move in and out. The more inflamed the airways are, the more difficult it is to breathe.

Some asthmatics have only minor breathing problems. For them, full-blown attacks happen very infrequently. But for others, the potential for a life-threatening asthma attack is a near-constant worry. Though asthma can't be cured, one way to get a handle on the condition is to be aware of its symptoms.

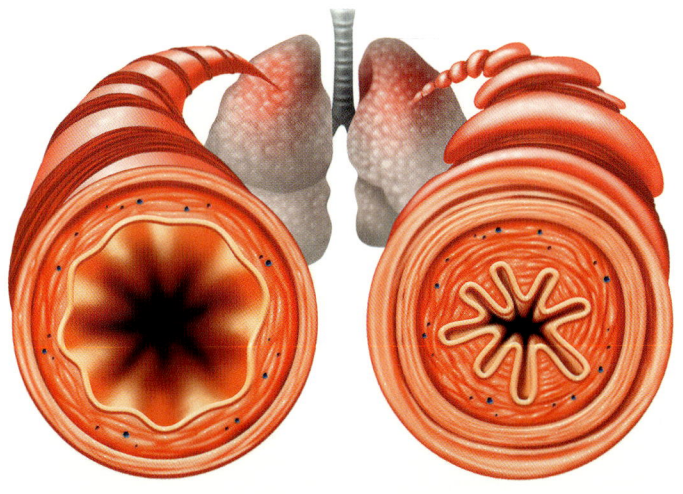

The left side of this image shows a normal airway in the lungs. The right side demonstrates its state during an asthma attack: swollen and filled with mucus, making it difficult to breathe.

Asthma Symptoms

Asthma symptoms vary from person to person. In some cases, they are mild to moderate. The most common symptoms include chest pain, shortness of breath, and wheezing. Coughing is also possible, most often in the early morning or late in the evening. These symptoms can cause insomnia, or trouble sleeping, and they can increase in intensity during an illness such as a flu or the common cold.

In more serious cases, symptoms can lead to severe respiratory distress or even death. Signs

Asthma and COVID-19

Beginning in late December 2019, a newly discovered respiratory disease called COVID-19 swept across the planet. It began in Wuhan, China, and quickly spread to more than 200 countries worldwide. It was caused by a virus called SARS-CoV-2 , which belongs to a family of viruses known as coronaviruses.

The vast majority of people who contract COVID-19 experience mild or no symptoms. Symptoms include fever, coughing, and shortness of breath, overlapping with the symptoms of asthma or the common cold. In severe cases, the disease can lead to pneumonia, the failure of multiple organs, and even death.

Asthma is a respiratory disease. Scientists believe that people with moderate to severe asthma therefore have a much higher risk of falling very ill if they contract COVID-19. Doctors in 2020 said the best way for asthmatics to prevent the illness was to remain isolated from other people in order to avoid contracting the virus.

of a serious asthma attack include extremely pronounced wheezing, rapid breathing, difficulty talking due to shortness of breath, and excessive sweating. Sometimes the skin can turn blue from lack of oxygen.

For adults, dealing with severe physical side effects can be worrisome. But in children who aren't always able to care for themselves on their own, it can be even more troubling. The symptoms of pediatric asthma include a nagging cough that can last for days or even weeks, fast breathing that tightens the skin around the ribs or neck, a runny nose, and recurrent chest colds that take longer than usual to go away.

Environmental Causes

It isn't fully clear why some people develop asthma and others don't. But there are a few theories as to why it occurs. Most doctors agree that asthma is caused by a combination of environmental and genetic factors.

Two of the main environmental causes of asthma are allergens and toxic substances in the air. When inhaled, things such as tree pollen, dust mites, mold spores, pet dander, and even microscopic particles

Asthma in Children

According to the American College of Allergy, Asthma, and Immunology, most children with asthma develop symptoms before they turn five. But because kids have smaller bronchial tubes and are more prone to catching illnesses such as head or chest colds that inflame these airways, it can be difficult for doctors to properly diagnose the condition in children. When trying to rule out short-term conditions such as bronchitis, hay fever, or the flu, one of the first symptoms doctors look for is a breathing cycle that is louder or faster than normal. For example, newborns take 30 to 60 breaths a minute under normal circumstances. Toddlers usually take 20 to 40 breaths a minute. A measurement that is higher than that might be a sign that asthma is the problem.

of cockroach droppings can cause airways to become inflamed. Workplace irritants, such as chemicals used in farming, hairdressing, and manufacturing, can also have this effect. Car exhaust is another harmful culprit. When inhaled in large quantities or even small quantities over a sustained period of time, these things can trigger symptoms or a full-blown attack.

Tobacco smoke, including secondhand smoke, is one of the most damaging contributors to asthma. "Smoking is an unhealthy habit for anyone, but it's especially bad for people who have asthma," writes pediatrician Dr. Elana Pearl Ben-Joseph. "Smoking makes the airways become swollen, narrow, and filled with sticky mucus—the same problems that cause

Tree pollen can be a significant seasonal contributor to asthma symptoms.

Asthma, Smoking, and Vaping

According to the CDC, tobacco smoke—including secondhand smoke—contains more than 7,000 chemicals.[3] This includes traces of poisons such as formaldehyde, arsenic, and cyanide. More than 70 of these ingredients can cause cancer. When breathed in, these toxins can also trigger an asthma attack by increasing mucus production, causing swelling in the bronchial tubes, and irritating the lungs.

Since the rise in using electronic cigarettes, or vaping, in recent years, a link between asthma and vaping has also been found. In 2019, a study published in the journal *BMC Pulmonary Medicine* surveyed 400,000 people who had never smoked regular cigarettes. Around 34,000 of them had asthma, and 3,100 of the participants vaped. The study found the risk of asthma was 39 percent higher in those who vaped than in those who had never done so.[4] The more people vaped, the greater their chances for developing asthma.

---

breathing trouble in people with asthma. For this reason, a smoker who has asthma is more likely to have more frequent and severe flare-ups."[2]

People often exercise to keep their bodies healthy and in shape, but intense physical activity can also be a major asthma trigger. For example, a brisk run in the park or a prolonged bike ride can cause inflammation in the lungs, shortness of breath, and other precursors to an asthma attack. "If you notice symptoms like wheezing or coughing while exercising, you may have exercise-induced bronchoconstriction, commonly referred to as exercise-induced asthma," writes asthma expert Dr. Pat Bass. "About 5 percent of the US population has exercise-induced asthma and will benefit from getting a diagnosis and the appropriate treatment."[5]

Some doctors have noticed that asthmatics who are generally healthy and don't smoke are less likely to have severe asthma attacks if they live at higher altitudes. For example, Denver, Colorado, is one of the most polluted cities in the United States. But the Asthma and Allergy Foundation of America named it one of the top 25 large US cities to live in for people who have asthma. According to Peter Hackett, who works at the Institute for Altitude Medicine in Telluride, Colorado, this is because Denver has thinner

> "There are dozens of papers about asthma and altitude, and in general asthmatics do better when they go to high altitudes. In fact, if you take urban children and take them to high altitudes for a while, their asthma improves. And if you take mountain kids and send them to an urban environment, their asthma gets worse."[6]
>
> —Peter Hackett of the Institute for Altitude Medicine, Telluride, Colorado

air due to its high altitude. Though the air is thinner and therefore has less oxygen, its thinness also makes it easier to breathe once a person has adjusted to the altitude.

Genetic and Biological Risk Factors

In addition to environmental factors, doctors believe genetics play a role in asthma development. Some people may be hereditarily predisposed to have poor reactions to certain substances, such as additives in food or beverages. For example, sulfites in wine and beer, as well as preservatives added to dried fruit and shrimp, are known asthma triggers. Certain medications, such as aspirin, ibuprofen (Advil), naproxen sodium (Aleve), and some types of beta-blockers, can also trigger an asthma attack.

Emotional and mental distress have been known to bring on asthma symptoms in some people who react particularly negatively to stress. Whether it's about doing well in school, dealing with a family or relationship problem, or even obsessing over when the next asthma episode might occur, ongoing stress can cause asthma symptoms to kick into overdrive. As the worrying increases, the coughing and wheezing get worse, making an attack all the

Asthma & GERD

Gastroesophageal reflux disease (GERD) is a condition in which acid from the stomach flows upward into the esophagus, the tube that connects the mouth to the stomach. It causes a burning feeling in the chest and usually happens after a meal. The burning feeling gets worse when lying down.

Scientists don't know whether GERD causes asthma or the other way around. But studies have shown that asthma and GERD often happen together and affect each other. In other words, asthma can make GERD seem more unbearable, and GERD can do the same for asthma. Aside from finding the right medicines to treat the two conditions, doctors suggest that people who suffer from both GERD and asthma should avoid triggers if at all possible. They recommend avoiding spicy or fatty food, alcohol, and cigarettes and e-cigarettes.

more likely. It's a cycle that can spiral out of control very quickly.

A growing body of research suggests that obesity can increase one's risk of developing asthma, especially in kids. A study of more than 500,000 kids published in December 2018 in the journal *Pediatrics* stated that overweight and obese children had a higher chance of developing asthma. Overweight children had an 8 to 17 percent higher risk of developing asthma compared to their non-overweight peers. Obese kids in the study were 26 to 38 percent more likely to develop asthma than those whose weight was within a healthy range. "The idea that obesity and asthma may be linked has become more widely accepted," says Beth A. Miller, MD, director of the UK HealthCare Asthma, Allergy, and Sinus Clinic.[7]

A person whose parent or close relative has asthma is more likely to develop the condition too. In fact, the American Lung Association reports that a person is three to six times more likely to have asthma if he or she has a parent who has asthma. But if a parent has asthma, it doesn't mean the children are guaranteed to get it. "Asthma can be genetic, though not all cases of asthma are inherited. Asthma has a range of other causes and risk factors," writes Jenna Fletcher, science writer for Medical News Today.[8]

Researchers have found evidence that obesity has a link with asthma.

Chapter *Three*

Getting a Diagnosis

Asthma affects more than 24 million people in the United States. It can be life-threatening, so it's important to address the issue head-on as soon as the symptoms start. Signs of a serious problem include a tight chest even when doing very little exercise or no physical activity at all, rapid worsening of wheezing or shortness of breath, and zero improvement after using a quick-relief inhaler.

While a person can receive an asthma diagnosis at any age, even as an adult, most people are told they have the condition when they are children. Doctors, whether they are pediatricians, internists, allergists, otolaryngologists, or pulmonologists, will use a variety of methods to come to a firm conclusion. This will include a full medical history review and a physical exam. During the exam, they'll look at the

Extreme difficulties breathing during even light exercise can be a sign that a person should see a doctor.

ears, eyes, nose, throat, skin, chest, and lungs for any abnormalities. If anything looks suspicious, they might do an X-ray to get a closer look.

Most physicians will also do a series of tests to rule out allergies and other conditions that imitate asthma and its symptoms. One such illness is called chronic obstructive pulmonary disease (COPD), a type of inflammatory lung

> "Perhaps you're not feeling positive now, but with time, support and advice, you can get there. Sometimes a diagnosis can be a starting point for finding out as much as you can about asthma and getting on top of symptoms."[1]
>
> —Kathy, a nurse who works for the Asthma UK Helpline

Preparing for the Appointment

Seeking professional medical help can be scary for any reason, especially when it's possible there might be news of a serious disease at the end of it. But doctors at the Mayo Clinic recommend preparing before the appointment by researching what to expect. They also suggest keeping a diary of symptoms, including dates, times, and severity levels. The diary should also record any exposure to pets, tobacco smoke, chemical fumes, mold, or dust. Finally, they advise patients to wear comfortable, nonrestrictive clothing in case any exercise tests are administered.

Asthma Misdiagnoses

According to Dr. Kyle Happel at the American College of Admissions, one of the most defining characteristics of asthma is the fact that its symptoms vary and fluctuate over time. "Asthma is a disease whose symptoms are caused by variable airflow obstruction. It varies throughout the day, usually, and certainly by the week or by the month," he says.[2] If a doctor diagnoses a patient with asthma because of a set of symptoms that remains constant over time, there is a chance it is a misdiagnosis.

There are many diseases and conditions with symptoms that mirror those of asthma. Some of the most common include COPD; gastroesophageal reflux disease (GERD); rhinosinusitis, an inflammation of the sinuses and naval cavity; angina, a type of chest pain caused by reduced blood flow to the heart; anxiety; and vocal cord dysfunction syndrome.

disease that causes obstructed airflow in the lungs. Patients are encouraged to ask questions during the diagnosis in order to better understand their condition and potential treatment.

Testing for Asthma

Doctors do a variety of exams when testing for asthma and its severity. First, they conduct pulmonary tests to determine how well the patient is breathing. In addition to a spirometry test, most physicians use a peak flow meter. In this test, the patient inhales deeply, then breathes out into a device

The Methacholine Challenge

The methacholine challenge, also referred to as the bronchoprovocation test, is a way to determine whether someone has asthma. During the exam, the patient inhales doses of methacholine, a drug that causes narrowing of the airways. It is supposed to mimic what happens during an asthma attack. After each dose, breathing is measured to determine how narrow the patient's airways are. If the patient experiences severe discomfort at any time, the test is over.

The test result is considered positive if the patient has a 20 percent or greater decrease in breathing ability compared to normal function. In this case, an asthma diagnosis is likely. If the patient's breathing patterns don't decrease after taking methacholine, asthma can most likely be ruled out as the problem.

that measures the force of the exhalation. A low peak flow reading is a signal that the patient's lungs aren't working properly and that uncontrolled asthma may be the problem.

Another method is called a nitric oxide test. It measures the amount of nitric oxide the patient has in her breath. Much like with the peak flow meter, the patient breathes into a device connected to a machine that provides a reading. Nitric oxide is a type of gas normally found in the body. But high levels can be a sign of inflamed airways and asthma.

Some doctors also like to administer exercise-related tests, especially if the patient is prone to symptom flare-ups after

Doctors can use spirometry to assess a patient's breathing capacity.

doing things like running or playing sports. The tests usually involve running on a treadmill for six to eight minutes while the patient's heart rate, oxygen levels, and heart rhythm are monitored. Spirometry tests are given before, during, and after the exercise to measure airflow. If symptoms appear, it is highly likely that exercise is an asthma trigger for the patient.

How Asthma Is Classified

Sometimes figuring out a health problem can be nerve-racking and time-consuming for the patient and the health-care team. But once the test results are back, doctors can study them to determine whether asthma is present, how serious it is, and what possible treatment options are. According to the Mayo Clinic, a leading US hospital, asthma can be classified into four major categories and asthmatics can move between categories at different stages in their lives. The first category is mild intermittent. People who have mild intermittent asthma usually exhibit mild

Diagnosing Asthma in Children Under Six

Diagnosing asthma in children can be tricky. Most children younger than six can't blow hard enough to register a result on a pulmonary function test. For these patients, most doctors will go through history and symptoms with the parent or guardian. Then they will do a physical exam, but without using a peak flow meter or spirometer. Depending on the results, some doctors will prescribe lower doses of asthma medication for a few months to see if the child's symptoms dissipate. According to the National Heart, Lung, and Blood Institute, approximately 40 percent of children who wheeze when they get colds or other types of respiratory infections are eventually diagnosed with asthma when they are old enough to be tested properly.[3]

symptoms for up to two days a week and two nights a month.

For patients who have mild persistent asthma, the coughing and wheezing happen more than twice a week but no more than once in a single day. People with moderate persistent asthma exhibit symptoms once a day and more than one night a week. Patients with the most serious symptoms have severe persistent asthma. This means they experience shortness of breath or general trouble breathing throughout the day on most days and also regularly at night.

According to the Allergy and Asthma Network, 5 to 10 percent of all asthma patients are affected by severe asthma.[4] One such

Nocturnal Asthma

One subtype of asthma is most often triggered at night. Doctors believe nocturnal asthma may be caused by hormone fluctuation during the sleep cycle. Another possible cause is acid reflux. When a person lies down, it's easier for acid in the stomach to travel up into the esophagus. This causes a blockage and triggers a cough. The more the person coughs, the greater the airways swell and the more likely an asthma attack becomes. A third possible cause of nocturnal asthma is a secondary condition, such as postnasal drip or a chronic sinus infection. During sleep, the airways narrow, which naturally increases airflow resistance. If there's any excess drainage from the nose, it could get in the way of breathing.

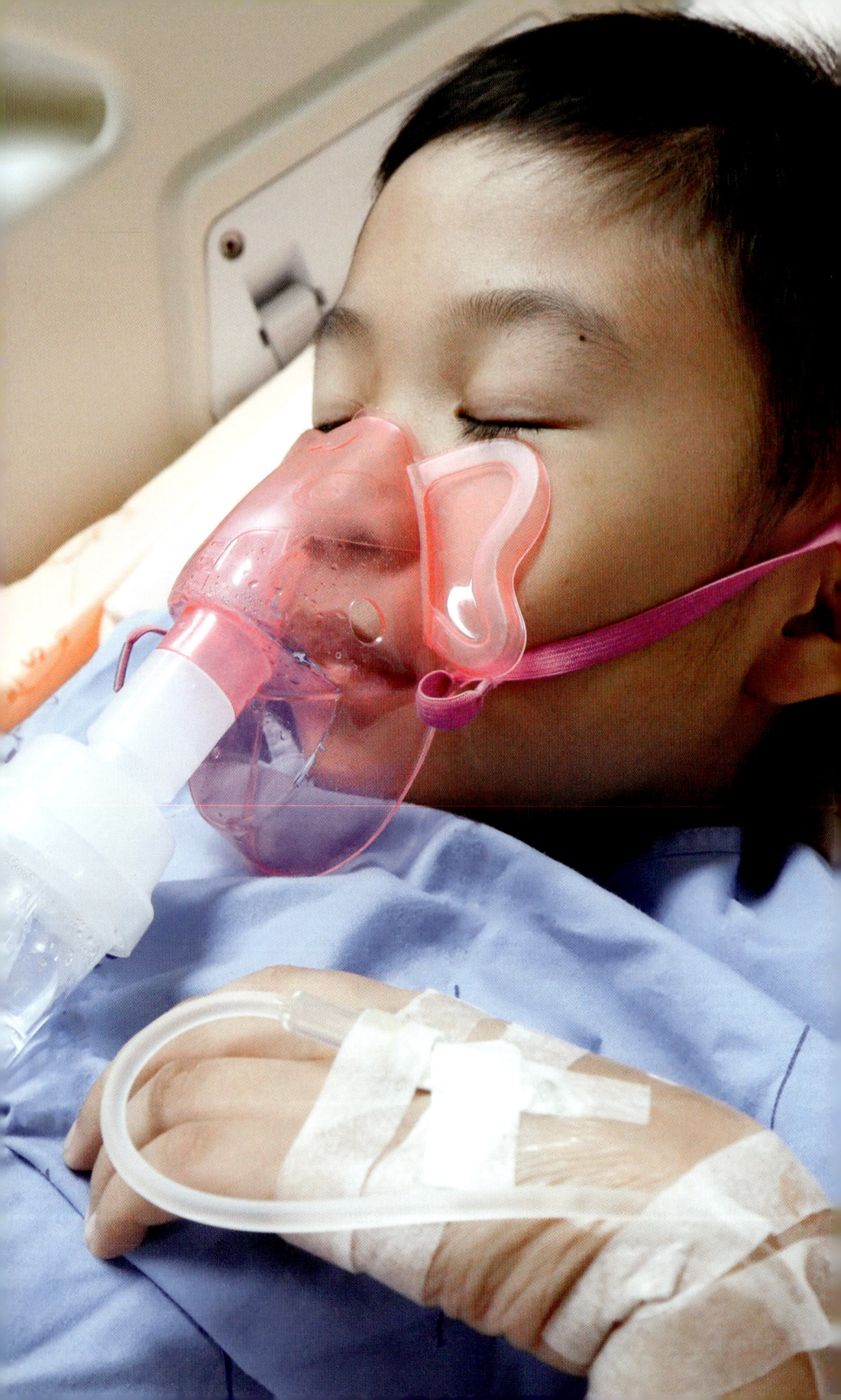

A severe asthma attack may require a trip to the hospital.

patient is Greg Hebrank of Jeanette, Pennsylvania. When Greg was ten years old, he woke up in the middle of the night suddenly unable to breathe. Though he had always suffered from seasonal allergies from pollen and dust, his breathing troubles had been mostly manageable. But by morning, the problem had gotten so bad that his mother panicked. "He just kept getting worse," says Chris Hebrank. "By morning, I was scared to death."[5]

Chris drove her son to the hospital. When they arrived, the doctors tried to determine Greg's lung function, but he was too weak to properly perform the peak flow test. They gave him drugs to try to open his airways but nothing worked. His lung function dropped so far and so rapidly that he had to receive all of his oxygen through a mask. The physicians transferred Greg to the intensive care unit (ICU)

> "After Greg was first diagnosed with asthma, for the first time he has been consistently sleeping through the night. And he's so much more active than ever before. He's constantly outside riding his bike, skateboarding, roller blading or playing soccer with friends. At night, I have to beg him to come in."[8]
>
> —Chris Hebrank, mother of a child with asthma

for round-the-clock monitoring. They also told Chris what they suspected: Greg had severe asthma, not allergies. "Until then, I thought Greg was having a severe allergic reaction. We never knew that Greg had asthma," Chris says.[6]

After two days in the ICU, more tests, and medication, Greg finally felt well enough to be released from the hospital. Chris was overjoyed. "The best thing that happened as a result of Greg's asthma attack was that we learned once and for all what we were dealing with and how to treat him," she says. "Until then, we had been treating Greg as a kid with severe allergies, and a lot of the things we were doing to help his allergies were actually making his asthma worse."[7]

Two weeks after his stay in the hospital, Greg's lung function was 80 percent of what it used to be. It soon rose to 90 and then 100 percent. At a follow-up doctor visit, the pediatrician suggested that Greg had likely had moderate to severe asthma for years but that it had gone undiagnosed. Greg now mostly uses a nasal spray to control his allergies. He also uses an inhaler to manage his daily asthma symptoms. Greg's story is not unique. Asthma affects kids and adults in countries all over the world.

Chapter *Four*

Disease Demographics

In 2012, representatives from countries all around the world got together to form an organization that aimed to study asthma and its effects on individuals. By 2020, the Global Asthma Network (GAN) had 381 centers in 137 countries worldwide.[1] By conducting research about the disease, publishing surveys on its prevalence, and working to improve access to quality care and medicines in low- and middle-income countries, the group strives to improve asthma care worldwide.

According to the GAN's 2018 Global Asthma Report, asthma is one of the most common noncommunicable diseases in the world. Though the World Health Organization (WHO) estimates the total number of people who suffer from asthma at 235 million, GAN suggests that as many

Asthma affects people of all ages, genders, and ethnicities.

> "Asthma does not have to be a burden or cause suffering."[5]
> —*Global Asthma Report, 2018*

as 339 million people of all ages and in all regions have the disease.[2] Asthma diagnoses are especially prevalent in English-speaking countries in Europe, Asia, and North and South America.

Asthma in the United States

Since the 1980s, asthma's prevalence has been increasing in all ages and all age groups. In 2018, more than 24 million people in the United States suffered from asthma, according to the CDC's figures. The highest rate is among people ages 15 to 19, while the lowest rate is among infants between the ages of newborn and four.[3] More than 11.4 million people with asthma, including nearly three million children, reported having had one or more asthma episodes or attacks in 2017.[4]

When looking at the population as a whole, asthma is more common in females than in males. Approximately 9.1 percent of females had the condition in 2018, compared to 6.2 percent of males. It was also more common in women ages 18 and older than in men of that same age range, affecting

Among most age groups, asthma affects females at a higher rate than males.

9.8 percent of women and 5.5 percent of men. The only population in which asthma affected males more than females was in kids 18 and younger.[6]

Though asthma impacts people of all races and ethnicities, African Americans are at a higher risk than people of other backgrounds. They are three times more likely to die from asthma than any other group. About 13.4 percent of African American children have asthma, compared to about 7.4 percent of white children. Though Hispanic people are less likely to have asthma than African Americans, white people, American Indians, and Alaska natives, the numbers vary within Hispanic ethnic groups. For example, Puerto Ricans (14 percent) are much more likely than Mexican Americans (5.4 percent) to have the condition.[7]

Mortality Rates

Most people who have asthma do not die from it, but it can still be a serious, life-threatening illness. According to a 2016 CDC survey, the disease accounted for approximately 9.8 million trips to doctor's offices that year.[8] Asthma remains among the top causes of hospitalization among children under 15.

In general, adults are four times as likely to die from asthma compared to children. But despite this fact, asthma is by no means a death sentence. In 2018, fewer than 3,500 people died from an asthma attack or related condition. Only 192 of those deaths were adolescents under 18.[9] In most cases, asthma turns fatal when the disease isn't adequately treated or the treatment plan isn't properly followed.

Unequal Access to Care

The disease is a financial burden not only on the country but on the individuals as well. People who suffer from asthma spend an average of about $1,830 annually on prescription drugs. They spend $640 on office visits, $529 on hospitalizations, $176 on hospital outpatient visits, and $105 for emergency room care. For people who have health insurance or a steady income, that sum, which comes to $3,280, might be manageable.[10] But for families with lesser means, the cost of paying for asthma management becomes a major financial stressor.

Studies have shown that the high cost of treating asthma disproportionately

> "Even for those with insurance, the urgent-care and emergency-room bills, the copays, the costs of tests and overnight stays, the regular cost of upgrading and maintaining asthma devices, and the cost of prescriptions that can often follow severe attacks wreak financial havoc."[11]
>
> —*Vann R. Newkirk II, journalist and asthmatic*

affects African American and Hispanic—mostly Puerto Rican—populations living in lower-income communities. They are at a greater risk of exposure to environmental triggers and residential allergens such as dust mites and mold. They also have less access to quality preventative care, a shortage of primary care physicians in their local area, and additional language and literacy hurdles if and when they do find suitable treatment. These socioeconomic disparities are the main reason why some African American or Puerto Rican asthmatics die from or suffer through more debilitating versions of the disease than their more affluent, privileged neighbors.

Language Barriers

In asthma treatment plans, it's important that patients fully understand not only the types of medication they are taking but also when and how often to take them. In communities where different languages are spoken, this can be extraordinarily difficult when the only doctor available is someone who exclusively speaks English. Language barriers can trigger a number of problems in treatment effectiveness, including a failure to fill medications, poor compliance with filled prescriptions, and missed follow-up appointments. Though US law requires hospitals that receive federal funds to provide access to all patients, which includes providing translation services, many hospitals do not.

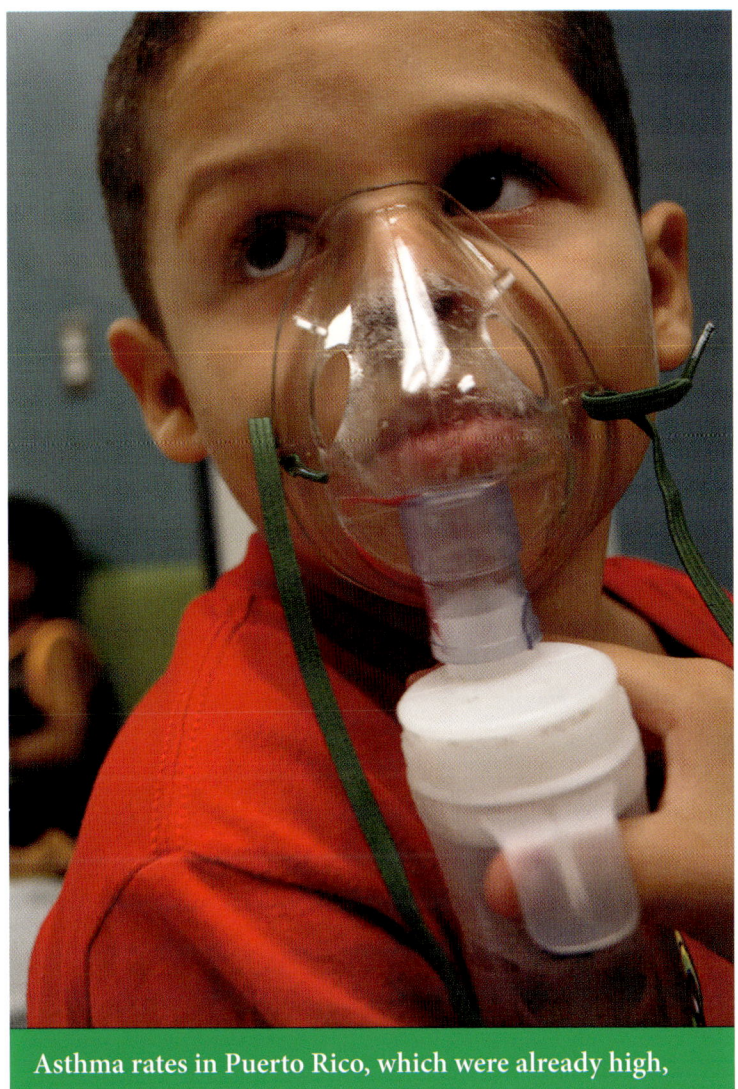

Asthma rates in Puerto Rico, which were already high, increased further following Hurricane Maria in 2017.

Some families distrust physicians because of a history of racial discrimination in health care. Others may speak a different language than their health-care providers, and in the absence of translators, they

Healthy Kids Express

At Saint Louis Children's Hospital in Saint Louis, Missouri, asthma is the top reason for patient admissions. It's also one of the most common reasons for emergency room visits. But doctors and health professionals noticed that a disproportionate number of patients from underserved communities weren't getting the necessary care. In response, they created Healthy Kids Express, a program that brings asthma experts to low-income and underprivileged neighborhoods in a big, brightly colored bus.

Healthy Kids Express provides informational pamphlets, books, and other resources to school nurses so they are better able to treat local children with asthma. The program visits doctors' offices in the area to make sure their equipment and asthma treatment plans are suitable. It also runs Asthma Control Education (ACE) classes in small-group settings for children and their caregivers to teach them about what causes asthma, what the environmental triggers are, and how to take asthma medication. The program is free.

may be unable to grasp the terms of treatment. Health-care resources that might be easily accessible to those in white, upper-class neighborhoods might not be readily available to people in minority areas.

Experts in the medical community are aware of this problem. Asthma education and management programs designed specifically for minorities have appeared in recent decades to help bridge the gap in care. Among other important goals, these culturally sensitive organizations teach people how to safely use inhalers and other preventative medications, explain why environmental factors such as dust and mold are so harmful to the respiratory system, and correct misconceptions about asthma medications and how effective they can be during treatment. Many of the programs are available in different languages, and some are geared toward children. Hospitals all over the country are trying to make more of these programs available to those who need them.

Chapter *Five*

The History of Asthma

Today's scientists know that asthma is a chronic disease caused by inflammation and blockages in the airways leading to the lungs. It has become more common in recent years. Since the 1980s, the number of cases in the United States has increased by roughly 60 percent, according to the WHO.[1] Despite advances in medicine and treatment options, the number of deaths has also risen. But asthma is not a new illness. In fact, experts believe the condition existed thousands of years ago.

Historians don't know for sure when and where asthma originated. But many trace its earliest recorded occurrence back to China in 2600 BCE, before the condition even had a name. Records reference a disorder characterized by noisy breathing, or wheezing. It's also mentioned in one of the oldest

> Hippocrates, a key figure in the history of medicine, was the first to use the term *asthma* to describe an illness defined by breathing difficulties.

The Stinking Nightshade Healing Method

The Ebers papyrus included a wide variety of advice, including instructions on how to ease the pain of a crocodile bite and explanations of how to get rid of rats, scorpions, or spiders in the home. Many remedies addressed airway blockage. One in particular suggested inhaling the vapor of the black henbane plant, otherwise known as the stinking nightshade. The advice was simple: Place the plant on hot bricks. Cover the plant with a jar that had a hole in it. Using a reed stalk as a straw, breathe in the vapors from the smoking plant to ease any chest pain or discomfort due to clogged airways. This method does not stand up to modern medical scrutiny, but in a way it was the forerunner of today's inhalers.

---

known medical texts, the Ebers papyrus, which dates back to about 1550 BCE. The scroll contains 700 formulas and remedies for various ailments, including breathing troubles.

The condition appeared again in the historical record in 460 BCE, this time in ancient Greece. Hippocrates, often referred to as the grandfather of modern medicine, linked the mysterious ailment to environmental triggers and specific types of work, such as metalwork. He called the disease *asthma*. The name comes from the Greek word *aazein*, which means to exhale with an open mouth, pant, or take in a sharp breath.

Though it now had a concrete name, asthma remained a vague concept for hundreds of years. Scientists, physicians, and religious theorists continued to define what the condition was and learn how it should be treated. In 100 CE, a Greek physician named Aretaeus of Cappadocia gave asthma an official definition similar to how the disease is described today. He wrote about a "thick and viscid phlegm caused by coldness and humidity of the [air that is breathed]," and he listed chest heaviness, tiredness, and difficulty breathing as some of the symptoms.[2] He also suggested that though females were more likely to contract the condition than males, men had a greater chance of dying from it, and children had the best chance for recovery.

Around the same time, the Romans were studying asthma too. In 50 CE, writer and natural philosopher Pliny the Elder found links between pollen and breathing difficulties. In his encyclopedia *The Natural History*, he advised sufferers to drink a concoction of red wine and

> "If from running, gymnastic exercises or from any other work, the breathing becomes difficult, it is called asthma."[3]
>
> —*Aretaeus of Cappadocia*

Early Asthma Remedies

Today in the age of modern medicine, asthma sufferers have the luxury of using state-of-the-art devices such as inhalers and at-home spirometers to manage their condition. But in ancient times, people had to rely on more primitive methods to treat their illnesses.

Aretaeus of Cappadocia advised asthma sufferers to drink a mixture made from owl's blood and red wine. In *The Natural History*, Pliny the Elder wrote that the most successful remedy was to drink the blood of wild horses or eat 21 millipedes soaked in honey. "Next to that, [donkey's] milk boiled with bulbs, the whey being the part used, with the addition of [a flowering plant called] nasturtium steeped in water and tempered with honey," he wrote. "The liver . . . of a fox, taken in red wine, or bear's gall in water, facilitate the respiration."[4]

animal parts to alleviate symptoms. Maimonides, a Jewish physician and scholar who lived during the 1100s CE, prescribed sleep, plenty of fluids, and bowls of chicken soup. But it wasn't until the 1800s when significant advances in asthma research were made.

New Knowledge and Costly Mistakes

During the 1800s, scientists built upon what many of their predecessors had done. One famous doctor and asthma sufferer, Henry Hyde Salter, wrote *On*

Asthma: Its Pathology and Treatment in 1860. It contained hundreds of case studies and suggestions for treatment to control an asthma attack, including hot, strong coffee. It also provided one of the first official definitions of asthma as "paroxysmal dyspnoea of a peculiar character, generally periodic with intervals of healthy respiration between the attacks," caused by "nervous action" and exposure to the dander of horses, cats, and other animals.[5]

Perhaps the biggest development in the study of asthma at that time came in 1892. That year,

Henry Hyde Salter: Asthma Pioneer

Henry Hyde Salter was born on November 2, 1823, in Poole, a town in southwestern England. He grew up to become one of the world's top authorities on asthma. In 1856, at the age of 33, he became the youngest fellow elected to the Royal College of Physicians and the youngest person elected to the Royal Society. Part of his celebrity was due to his research and the hundreds of case studies he conducted in order to better understand the disease. But it was also because he suffered from asthma himself and had a keen understanding of the condition.

Salter developed asthma as a baby after a serious case of whooping cough. Though the asthma was severe throughout his childhood, it dissipated in his early adult years, and he lived a productive, fruitful life. Unfortunately, when he was 44, the illness came back with a vengeance. In 1871, he contracted a bacterial infection called typhoid and developed a growth on his lung. Salter died on August 31 of that year at the age of 48.

Sir William Osler became interested in studying the disease. Osler, one of the cofounders of the Johns Hopkins Medical School, is often referred to as the father of modern medicine. He defined some of the parameters for asthma that still exist today, such as

Sir William Osler did important research on asthma, but he was unable to determine its exact cause, resulting in ineffective treatments.

The Evolution of Inhalers

Inhalers are a key method of treating asthma today. But they weren't always such tiny portable devices. The first inhaler was created in 1778 by inventor John Mudge. It was a teapot-like vessel made out of pewter that had tiny holes in the top. People would pour boiling water and medicinal herbs into the pot, close the lid, and breathe in the steam through a flexible tube sticking out from an opening in the cover.

During the 1800s, the first portable nebulizer, a type of machine that released asthma medication, was invented. It was called the Pulverisateur. The pump handle forced liquid medicine through an atomizer—a device used to spray out water, perfume, or other liquids—and turned it into a vapor. Around the same time, dry powder inhalers also became popular, including the carbolic smoke ball. Users squeezed a rubber ball. This pushed a fine carbolic acid powder through a strainer and converted it into an inhalable spray. Although the invention promised to cure asthma in ten minutes, in reality it was ineffective.

the definition of the disease as a series of bronchial spasms. Osler noted the similarities between asthma and allergic conditions, such as hay fever. He connected asthma to genetics, stating that the illness ran in families and began in childhood. He also confirmed the specific triggers of asthma, including weather, extreme emotion or stress, and diet.

But despite these breakthroughs, Osler made one major error. He presumed that the blockage of airways during an asthma attack happened because of muscle spasms in the bronchial tubes, not because of inflammation. This caused doctors to prescribe over-the-counter drugs called bronchodilators to calm these spasms. The bronchodilators worked to relieve short-term symptoms. But they didn't address the deeper problem with the immune system, which meant people still died from the disease. Deaths from asthma attacks and asthma-related illnesses surged until the late 1900s.

Modern Research

In 1969, the Food and Drug Administration (FDA) limited the use of over-the-counter bronchodilators. Beginning in the 1970s, doctors started focusing on inflammation and the body's immune system. They conducted clinical trials to study the effectiveness of corticosteroids and other medications to reduce inflammation in the lungs and treat both the short- and long-term effects of asthma.

> "If you look at where asthma was in 1965 versus now, lots of people before were basically disabled or worse. Therapies are much better now, and there are so many [treatment] options to choose from."[6]
>
> —*Tod Olin, pediatric pulmonologist*

Martin Wright's peak flow meters helped improve the diagnosis of asthma.

In 1970, Dr. Martin Wright invented a peak flow meter known as the Mini Wright. It turned out to be extremely helpful for asthma research. Unlike a previous model he created nearly 20 years earlier, this version was both inexpensive and portable. It enabled doctors to get more accurate test results when diagnosing asthma. People at home could also use the device to help predict when an asthma attack might occur.

Over the next 50 years, doctors' attitudes toward treating asthma shifted. In addition to advances in medications and technological devices such as pressurized canisters and dry powder dispensers, medical professionals started promoting preventative care rather than just treating the symptoms when they occurred. This meant producing drugs that could be used daily during a particularly aggressive allergy season, during multiple seasons to prevent flare-ups, or even year-round depending on the severity of the asthma.

The rise of the internet in the early 2000s played an indirect but nonetheless important role in asthma research and treatment. More information can now be shared quickly between doctors, families, and patients. People can use apps and devices alongside traditional asthma treatments to help manage their condition. One such device is called the Aluna Spirometer, a portable device designed for kids ages

Asthma Apps

In addition to coming up with new devices, engineers and computer experts are working to come up with useful, engaging new smartphone apps for asthmatics. An app called Propeller receives information from a small sensor clipped to an inhaler. It allows users to keep track of data about where and when the inhaler is used, as well as information about humidity, temperature, and air quality.

The app Asthma MD allows users to keep track of their asthma activity, medications, and triggers in a digital diary. The data is then collected and transformed into a colorful graph that physicians can view in order to review and tweak treatment when necessary.

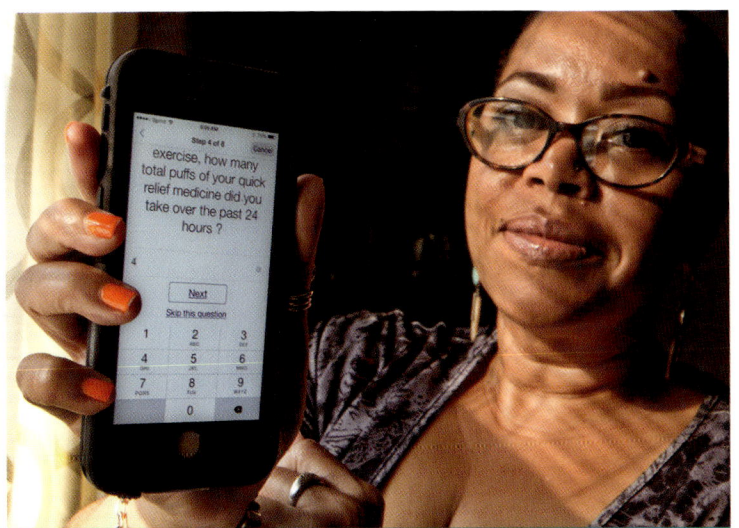

A patient with asthma demonstrates the app she uses to keep track of her symptoms and treatment.

five and older. It works much like a peak flow meter does. The child blows forcefully into the spirometer, which sends the measurement directly to an app. Parents, caregivers, and health-care providers can download results from the child's spirometry test at any time. They can also sign up to receive real-time alerts. There is even an interactive game on the app that encourages kids to use the device regularly.

Chapter *Six*

Asthma and Physical Health

High school sophomore Jonathan Rivera was 16 in 2019. He seemed to have everything going for him. He had a close-knit group of friends, loved to play basketball, and did well in school. But Jonathan's life wasn't always so stable. He spent much of his childhood in and out of doctors' offices and hospital emergency rooms. When he was just four years old, he was diagnosed with severe asthma.

"It hasn't been easy growing up with asthma," Jonathan said during an interview for National Asthma and Allergy Awareness Month. "When I was doing something fun, like running, when I was playing sports, and I started coughing or got short of breath, I would have to stop myself. Sometimes it can get pretty bad."[1]

People with asthma can enjoy everyday physical activities, including sports, when they receive effective treatment.

> "Acute asthma patients can find themselves coughing all night. The shortness of breath and chest tightness can be severe enough where just trying to get out of bed can be really difficult."[3]
>
> *—Dr. Renee Riddle, pediatric specialist*

In addition to struggling with chest pain and debilitating bouts of wheezing, Jonathan rarely was able to get a good night's sleep. Though he had surgery to get his tonsils and adenoids removed and enrolled in sleep studies to ease his breathing issues, nothing seemed to make enough of an impact. He always felt exhausted and weak. "He has missed a lot of school over the years, and when he was there, like in gym class for example, his inhaler always had to be nearby," said Veronica Montalvo, Jonathan's mom, who also suffers from asthma.[2]

But when Jonathan turned 12, he and his health-care team turned a corner. His doctors prescribed a corticosteroid-based inhaler that Jonathan could use to manage his symptoms. Unlike the devices he had used in the past, which gave him only temporary relief and didn't do anything to solve the problem in the long term, this one had the right combination of medicines to keep his asthma attacks at bay for an extended period of time. "Jonathan and his family recognize his symptoms immediately now. They know what triggers to avoid," said pediatric specialist Renee Riddle, Jonathan's doctor. "He's playing basketball regularly and enjoying his life much more."[4]

Thanks to the effectiveness of his treatment, Jonathan is now able to invest in his daily activities. He can think about the future without worrying about whether asthma will prevent him from accomplishing his goals. "It is a whole lot better now,"

Effects on Sleep

Steve is a patient in his sixties who suffers from severe asthma. He's been admitted to the hospital for asthma-related emergencies more than 140 times. He's been intubated and put on a ventilator 50 times for respiratory fatigue or failure. And he has had four surgeries to repair and dilate his upper airway so air could get through.[5]

One of the most disturbing daily side effects Steve has had to deal with is lack of sleep. "I'm lucky if I stay asleep for more than an hour or two at a time. The reason being is that it's difficult to stay [asleep] when your airways are constantly closing up," Steve writes in his award-winning blog, BreathinStephen. "Severe asthma, like many lung conditions, doesn't just affect one's breathing. It has an impact on almost every aspect of that person's life. And it's usually in ways that most people either wouldn't think of, or would probably take for granted . . . like sleep."[6]

Jonathan says. "Even my friends know when we are hanging out what kind of things I need to avoid. I am starting to think about what I can do after I finish high school. I just breathe in and breathe out much easier and take each day as it comes."[7]

Exercise-Induced Asthma

For many people like Jonathan, asthma wreaks havoc on the body. In addition to disrupting one's sleep patterns, it can severely impact a person's ability to exercise. In fact, 90 percent of people with the condition have exercise-induced bronchoconstriction, more commonly referred to as exercise-induced asthma.[8] This is when exercise

Exercise Tips

In addition to choosing low-impact workouts, there are steps one can take to stay physically active and prevent an asthma attack. Experts provide several tips for people with asthma who want to exercise. Don't exercise on days when the asthma is not under control. And don't exercise outside on days on which the pollen count or pollution is high. Or, find a way to exercise indoors. People should warm up and cool down for ten minutes before and after exercise, and they can use a rescue inhaler prior to exercising as a quick-relief treatment for symptoms and to stave off any attack. During exercise, they should try not to breathe through the mouth. Instead, they can inhale through the nose to humidify the air before it enters the lungs.

Long-distance running is one strenuous activity that can narrow the airways, creating exercise-induced asthma.

causes a narrowing of the airways, resulting in symptoms such as wheezing.

Factors that may increase the likelihood of an asthma-related episode include cold air, dry air, air pollution, and the chlorine used in swimming pools. Athletes who participate in activities that require extended periods of deep breathing through the mouth, such as long-distance running or soccer, are especially at risk.

In addition to too much exercise endangering asthma sufferers' health, a lack of physical activity can set in motion some major health problems too. People who are too sedentary and don't move around enough throughout the day can become overweight or obese. This can lead to more health issues down the road, such as heart problems, high cholesterol, diabetes, and a heightened risk of stroke.

But rather than stopping workouts altogether, doctors recommend that asthma patients choose sports that are more conducive to their condition. Activities that use short bursts of exercise, such as baseball, volleyball, or gymnastics, are healthier options. Walking, nonintense hiking, yoga, or a leisurely bike ride are also good choices. Sports done in cold, dry weather, such as ice-skating, ice

> "Warming up well before competing in sports can also reduce the risk of asthma symptoms developing during competition, in addition to reducing your risk of injury. If you're diagnosed with exercise-induced asthma and prescribed an inhaler, that inhaler should be with you at all times so that you have immediate access."[9]
>
> —Dr. Jonathan Parsons, pulmonologist

hockey, skiing, or snowboarding, should be avoided if at all possible without the proper medication or protective mask.

Occupational Asthma

Another type of asthma is related specifically to work. Called occupational asthma, it's caused by breathing in toxic fumes from chemicals, gases, or sprays found on the job. According to the American Academy of Allergy Asthma & Immunology, occupational asthma is the most common work-related lung disease in developed countries. People with allergies or those who have a family history of allergies are more likely

Toxic Triggers

According to the CDC, more than 300 workplace substances can be classified as triggers for asthma.[10] Some are encountered in animal-related professional environments. These substances include latex, certain types of antibiotics, and animal proteins from fur, saliva, urine, and dander. Others are found in hair salons or beauty supply stores. These include hair dye, formaldehyde, bleaching agents, and henna. Still others are found on industrial, manufacturing, or construction sites. Epoxy, resin, adhesives, metal dusts, wood dust or bark, and metalworking fluid fall into this category. Some of the most widespread examples pop up on farms and food production warehouses or restaurants. In these places people risk exposure to egg protein, green coffee bean dust, fish and shellfish, natural rubber latex, insects, and pollen.

> Sawdust generated by cutting wood is one example of a material that can contribute to asthma.

to develop occupational asthma than those whose families are allergy free.

Occupational asthma can result from repeated interaction with a substance that causes an allergic or immunologic response. For example, a person who works in a bakery and is allergic to flour might develop asthma and lung irritation due to long-term contact with the powdery substance. Someone with a sensitivity to latex might develop asthma from working in a job where the material is often present, such as a veterinarian's office, a doctor or dentist's office, a pipeline factory, or even certain mattress production plants. A person who is allergic to dust might want to think twice about beginning a career as a construction worker, carpenter, or house cleaner.

Occupational asthma can progress over time. As with other types of

Workers who paint cars must wear protective gear to guard against inhaling toxic substances.

asthma, the symptoms increase with exposure. They might get worse as the workweek progresses, then recede during the weekend. The longer a person is around the aggravating substance, the more likely it is that he or she will develop long-lasting or potentially permanent asthma-related health problems. In some cases, having contact with toxic airborne triggers can cause permanent changes in the lungs, resulting in disability or even death. "The lungs are complex organs," says Philip Harber, a professor of public health at the University of Arizona in Tucson. "Occupational and environmental exposures can lead to scarring or fibrosis, asthma, COPD, and infection or cancer."[10]

While it's certainly possible to wear protective gear and bring an inhaler to work in hopes of preventing any breathing-related emergencies, many doctors suggest becoming familiar with asthma triggers and symptoms in order to avoid certain professions altogether. For example, auto body spray-painting creates a particularly toxic environment because of the prevalence of chemicals known as isocyanates. "It's frequently a career-ending disease where [people] need to leave their profession," says Harber about asthma.[11]

Asthma affects all aspects of life. It disrupts sleep patterns, interferes with workouts and sports, and influences career choices. The condition can also pose a significant threat to a person's mental and emotional stability if left untreated.

Chapter *Seven*

Asthma and Mental Health

Whether it's planning for a big event such as a wedding or graduation, managing day-to-day tasks such as finishing homework, preparing for a job interview, or even paying bills, life can seem overwhelming at times. Managing the highs and lows is tricky enough even for people who are completely healthy. But for those who suffer from asthma, any type of extreme emotion—stress and anxiety, intense anger, even euphoric joy—can trigger an attack.

   Alex, a high school student in England, was diagnosed with asthma as a kid. Ever since then, he has struggled to manage his condition while maintaining the ability to live what he considered to be a normal life. "Through constant medication and making sure I'm doing stuff that isn't too strenuous, I've managed to keep [my asthma] down," he said in

> For someone already dealing with a hectic school or work life, asthma can add yet another layer of stress.

a 2017 interview with the British Lung Foundation on World Asthma Day. "But occasionally it does rear its head, and I get a really ugly reminder of how dangerous it can be. And on those occasions, things will go very wrong very, very quickly."[1]

In 2016, Alex was hospitalized after a severe asthma attack and spent four weeks out of school. When he returned home from the hospital, he was less able to participate in things like sports and any activity that required intense physical exercise. Before long, he noticed that his peers started to treat him differently. He got picked last for team games during gym class. When his friends got together to go bike riding or play a pickup game of soccer in the park, they didn't ask Alex to come along. That not only caused Alex anxiety but also hurt his feelings.

> "The greatest challenge I face when it comes to living with asthma is the effect it has on what I do. It creates this . . . mentality in people around me that I won't be able to do as well as they can. And I'm being sometimes put down by other people. . . . That does hurt sometimes."[2]
>
> —Alex

Unable to participate in certain activities, people with severe asthma may begin to feel left out.

    Alex worked with his doctors to come up with an exercise and medication plan that would build up his immune system without putting his lungs at risk. Over time, he was able to rejoin the cricket and rugby teams, and he could again go cycling on the weekend with friends. "The fact that I began exercising more and more meant that my cardiovascular system got better and better," Alex said. "Nowadays I can do lots of sports and I won't always have an asthma attack . . . I [feel] very confident . . . that asthma [isn't] something that [will] hold me back for the rest of my life."[3]

Asthma can limit a person's ability to participate in meaningful activities and strip away his confidence in his ability to maintain solid relationships. As a result, the disease can seriously impact a person's mental and emotional well-being. One of the riskiest asthma triggers is stress.

Stress-Induced Asthma

People may experience anxiety over doing well on a standardized test or completing a college application. They may feel

> ## World Asthma Day
>
> World Asthma Day is an event organized by the Global Initiative for Asthma (GINA) that happens on the first Tuesday of May. Its goal is to improve asthma awareness and care around the world. The initiative started in 1998 in Barcelona, Spain. Asthma educators and health groups from 35 countries participate in the day.
>
> The theme of World Asthma Day 2019 was "STOP for Asthma," which stood for Symptom evaluation, Test response, Observe, assess, then Proceed to adjust treatment. In collaboration with the National Institutes of Health (NIH), GINA organized camps across the globe that offered free checkups. Doctors at the camps could help diagnose, treat, and provide advice for asthma patients.

anger bubbling over during a fight with a partner or spouse. They may fear for a loved one who is ill. Each of these emotions can cause a significant amount of stress. That stress can trigger an asthma attack. "It's long been suspected that emotions can make asthma symptoms worse," says psychiatrist Glenda MacQueen. "If you look back in history, Hippocrates said that people who have what we now call asthma should stay away from strong emotions."[4]

But it isn't the feeling itself that sparks the onset of asthma symptoms. Instead, it's the subtle inhalation and exhalation changes that take place during the

Asthma and Mental Illness

Anxiety is one of the main triggers of asthma symptoms. But the reverse can be true too. Living with asthma can cause undue stress on the individual, triggering anxiety. In fact, many asthmatics suffer from bouts of sadness, insecurity, and depression because they can't participate in the activities they cherish, are unable to compete on equal footing at work or school, or are seen as lacking by their peers.

Andrew G. Weinstein, an associate clinical professor of pediatrics at Thomas Jefferson Medical College, pushes his asthma patients to remain involved in their lives as much as possible, even if it means dealing with a little awkwardness or discomfort. "Many patients will have issues of depression," he says. "We have to find out their interests and encourage them to get back at it."[5]

strong emotion that cause muscles to constrict and the breathing rate to increase. In other words, anxiety can cause a person to hyperventilate, or breathe rapidly. The more the person hyperventilates, the greater the likelihood that wheezing, chest pain, or coughing will occur. Once those symptoms are set into motion, it can be harder to prevent a full-blown asthmatic episode from happening.

Research has shown that anxiety can also release an excess of histamine, the chemical that causes allergies. A heightened level of histamines in the body can cause the throat to tighten and block airflow. "[This] means that in addition to getting good medical care, people who have asthma

Stress and the Immune System

When people get upset or stressed, their bodies go through a number of significant changes. They might sleep too much or not at all. They might overeat or stop eating altogether. Crying also increases mucus production, which makes breathing more difficult.

In addition, stress can weaken the immune system, which protects the body against foreign bacteria and viruses. This not only worsens asthma symptoms but increases the person's vulnerability to asthma attacks and other more lethal infections. Some doctors have prescribed allergy shots or antihistamines for preventative relief. These can prevent asthma-aggravating symptoms, such as a runny nose, congestion, and watery eyes.

should pay attention to their psychological state, particularly those who have asthma that is difficult to control," says Michael Blumenfield, professor of psychiatry at New York Medical College.[6] The lower the stress, the lower the risk of an asthma attack.

Asthma and Relationships

In 2017, the Asthma and Allergy Foundation of America conducted a study called "My Life with Asthma." It polled more than 800 people online to see how asthma affected their lives. A majority of respondents said that asthma made them feel "frustrated and anxious." A large portion of people also said it made them feel

> "My kids are all adults now, but I look back on all of the years of allergy shots, After Hours visits, Urgent Care visits, ER visits and hospitalizations and wonder what it would have been like to have three healthy kids. . . . Yes, I'm still resentful of families with healthy children, because it was incredibly stressful and scary trying to keep my kids healthy and breathing. And I have a full head of grey hair to prove it!"[7]
>
> —*Andrea, "My Life as an Asthma Mom" blogger*

"annoyed, afraid, angry, and isolated" on any given day.[8] The condition influenced how they performed at work and at school. It also affected how they interacted with their significant others or members of their families.

But asthma doesn't just disrupt the life of the person who has it. It also affects family members, caregivers, friends, and coworkers, who are willingly or unwillingly along for the ride and might not know how to help. As many as 60 percent of participants with severe uncontrolled asthma reported that their condition scared their loved ones. Approximately 55 percent said it had negative consequences in their relationships with their spouses or significant others and friends. Only 17 percent said the disease had no impact on their relationships at all.[9]

"Siblings of kids with asthma may feel guilty, thinking that somehow they have caused the illness," writes Verywell Health reporter Carol Sorgen. "They also may be jealous or angry because of the additional attention their sibling receives, or they may be afraid that they may get asthma themselves. Some may also feel embarrassed by the symptoms that their sibling displays."[10]

Asthma and Personal Relationships

In 2017, the Asthma and Allergy Foundation of America's "My Life with Asthma" study asked respondents which of their personal relationships were affected by asthma. The results were divided into those with severe asthma and those with not-severe asthma.[11]

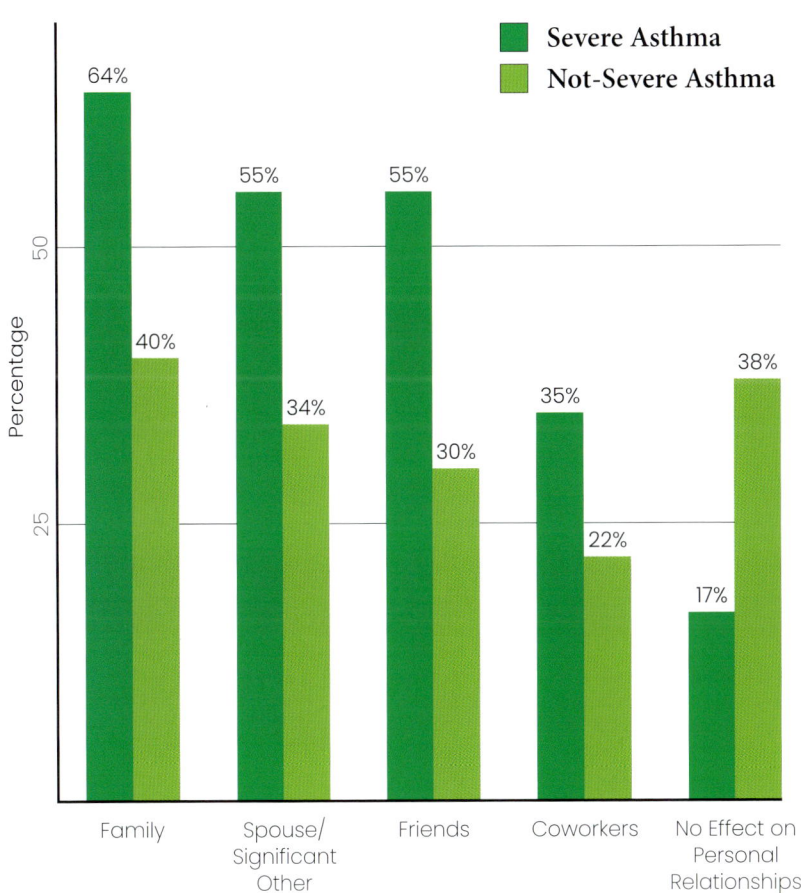

Parents might feel overwhelmed by the time and financial burden of the disease. Facing all the doctor appointments, trips to the pharmacy, and time it takes to fill out health insurance forms can be a challenge. "Managing asthma successfully takes time," Sorgen writes.[12]

But as with any health condition, there are tools family members or friends can take advantage of to help them handle the condition effectively without piling onto their own stress. There are local in person

Support groups, whether in person or online, can aid the family members of people with asthma as they try to help their loved ones.

support groups that are geared specifically toward helping family members or loved ones of people dealing with asthma. The Asthma and Allergy Foundation of America has a national hotline that caregivers can call for tips and information on the latest asthma research. Plus, doctors' offices are always great resources for support during the treatment process.

"Learning about [your loved one's] asthma (what treatments to take and when, what triggers to avoid and when) can be the hardest part of asthma care," writes pulmonologist Okan Elidemir. "[But] don't be discouraged. Learn as much as you can, talk to others living with asthma, read up on asthma, and discuss any concerns with [a] doctor."[13]

Chapter *Eight*

Treatment and Beyond

For many people, asthma is a lifelong condition that takes time and dedication to manage. But depending on the severity of the case, there are many treatment options available. It just takes a little patience in figuring out which plan works best. "I have seen tremendous benefits when a patient understands his or her disease, grasps the concept of airway inflammation, and then uses this knowledge to control it," says Dr. Thomas Ardiles, a board-certified internist with Banner University Medical Center in Phoenix. "Once our patients engage in their care, they see the greatest benefit."[1]

The first step in getting the best treatment is coming up with a suitable asthma action plan with a health-care provider. This is a written document that contains information on the symptoms as well

Patients can work with their doctors to develop asthma action plans.

as peak flow measurements that indicate the asthma is getting worse. The document also includes a list of things to do if there's an emergency. It should include telephone numbers for loved ones to contact in an emergency, a primary care physician or other doctor, and the local hospital. The asthma action plan also keeps track of which medications to take and when.

Treatment usually depends on the patient's age, asthma severity, and response to a given medication option. In most cases, this means a combination of long-term medicines that are taken daily to control and prevent asthma symptoms, along with quick-relief medicines that directly treat asthma episodes when they occur. As their name suggests,

Two Types of Inhalers

Depending on their preferences, asthma patients have two types of inhalers to choose from when treating their condition. The first is called a metered dose inhaler (MDI). It features a plastic container with a pressurized aerosol canister inside. The patient holds the plastic piece up to the mouth and pushes down on the canister. This releases a short burst of medicine into the mouth that then travels to the lungs.

The second option is called a dry powder inhaler (DPI). This device releases medicine in a fine powder that is then inhaled. Much like the MDI, it is small and portable. The difference with this inhaler is that it doesn't contain any propellants or other ingredients. The only thing inside the DPI is the medicine.

these medications provide quick relief and are only taken if needed.

Some asthma medications come in pill form or liquid form that reaches the airways through the bloodstream. But most are ingested using an inhaler or a tubed device called a nebulizer that takes liquid medicine and turns it into a mist that is then inhaled. Inhalers and nebulizers allow the medicine to go directly into the lungs for rapid relief.

Long-Term Medications

There are many types of long-term medications to choose from in order to keep asthma under control. The most popular and effective kinds are inhaled corticosteroids, such as fluticasone (Flovent), budesonide (Pulmicort Flexhaler), and flunisolide (Aerospan HFA). They reduce the body's

> "Inhaled steroids are one of the most effective medications [for treating asthma]. In general, these invaluable medications are not usually associated with side effects, and when they are, [side effects] are often quite mild."[2]
>
> —*Clifford W. Bassett, MD, founder and medical director of Allergy & Asthma Care of New York*

inflammatory response and mucus in the lungs. Though these might take anywhere from a few days to a few weeks to work effectively, they are low-risk, have few side effects, and are generally safe to use over a long period of time.

Leukotriene modifiers are another option. These oral medications in pill or liquid form block the

Like other inhaled steroids, budesonide helps decrease inflammation and swelling to clear airways.

body's normal response to leukotrienes, which are compounds released by the body as a response to allergens. For example, when someone who is allergic to pollen takes a walk outside, her body might release leukotrienes that cause her airway muscles to tighten. If she takes a leukotriene modifier, it might block this response, reduce inflammation, and allow her airways to open so she can breathe. In rare cases, leukotriene modifiers can cause psychological reactions, such as hallucinations, aggression, or depression.

Two other long-term options are long-acting beta agonists and theophylline. When inhaled, long-acting beta agonists open the airways by relaxing the smooth muscles surrounding them. They should

Bronchial Thermoplasty

Surgery isn't often recommended as a treatment for asthma. But there are procedures, such as bronchial thermoplasty, that have provided relief for some sufferers. Surgery is only used in severe cases where corticosteroids or other treatments haven't worked.

Bronchial thermoplasty is completed over the course of three outpatient visits. The procedure is fairly simple. The airways in the lungs are slowly heated using an electrode. This reduces the amount of smooth muscle inside the airways. It also limits the airways' ability to tighten or constrict. This makes breathing easier and possibly reduces the likelihood of asthma attacks over the long term.

only be used in combination with an inhaled corticosteroid. Theophylline is a pill or liquid that is taken daily. It also serves as a muscle relaxer around the airways but isn't prescribed as often as some of the other medications.

Quick-Relief Medications

Just like with long-term medications, there are plenty of options for fast-acting, short-term relief when it comes to asthma medications. These can be used during a symptom flare-up. They may also be used

Can Allergy Medications Treat Asthma Symptoms?

Not all asthmatics suffer from seasonal allergies. But for those who do, medications that aim to knock out allergy symptoms can work well when included in the treatment plan. In addition to over-the-counter drugs, allergy shots are an option. They work by gradually reducing the immune system's reaction to specific allergens, such as pollen. The shots are given on a weekly basis over the course of a few months. The regimen is then tapered down to a shot once a month for a period of three to five years.

For people with severe asthma who also suffer from serious allergies, a type of drug designed to reduce sensitivities to allergens is another option. One example is called omalizumab (Xolair). The medicine is distributed by injection every two to four weeks. While this prescription drug has been proven to be effective, it also alters the immune system and leaves the patient more susceptible to viruses and other illnesses.

before exercise if recommended by a doctor to relax tight muscles around the airways. The most popular and widely used are called short-acting beta agonists, such as albuterol (ProAir HFA or Ventolin HFA) and levalbuterol (Xopenex). The medicine is delivered using a handheld inhaler or nebulizer.

Other useful medications are called anticholinergics. Similar to short-acting beta agonists, these are inhaled, but they act more slowly. One example is ipratropium (Atrovent). It relaxes the airways and halts mucus production to make breathing easier.

A third option is to take an oral or intravenous corticosteroid such as prednisone or methylprednisolone. While these drugs also work to reduce and relieve airway inflammation, they are known to cause serious side effects, including insomnia, aggression, and an irregular heartbeat, when they are used for a long time. Because of this, they are usually prescribed only when absolutely necessary.

Experimental Treatments and Beyond

For most people, a personalized combination of short- and long-term medication provides ample

AGC Biologics is among the large, multinational companies now developing new biologic therapies.

support when it comes to keeping their asthma symptoms at bay and their attacks under control. Still, doctors and other health-care professionals are searching for new ways to improve treatment outcomes. They want to help patients who have exhausted all other options.

One up-and-coming field is called biologic therapy. Unlike other medications, which attempt to eliminate the effects of a symptom after it occurs, biologics target specific types of antibodies, molecules, or cells in the body that are causing the problem. Tiny particles are taken from the cells of a

Mena's Biologic Therapy

For years, 17-year-old Mena suffered from severe asthma, and nothing had worked to reduce her symptoms or her nagging allergies. In her freshman year of high school, she missed nearly six weeks of school after landing in the emergency room due to an asthma attack. Her doctors prescribed a hefty regimen of high-dose steroids, but they weren't as effective as they had hoped.

Then Mena's doctors suggested she try biologic therapy. They gave her a series of injections every three to four weeks. It reduced the inflammation in Mena's chest, allowing her to breathe more easily. "Mena used to get sick as soon as school started and then miss a week," says Mena's mom. "Now, even if she does get sick, we noticed she's only out of school for a day or two.... She gets better on her own and we don't have to rely on constant antibiotics."[3]

living organism, such as bacteria or mice. Then they are modified to target specific molecules in humans, such as antibodies, inflammatory molecules, or cell receptors. Biologics work by blocking the pathways that lead to inflammation in the first place. In addition to biologic therapy, many hospitals and organizations, such as the Mayo Clinic and the National Heart, Lung, and Blood Institute, are staging clinical trials in the hopes of either fine-tuning existing treatments or discovering new protocols to better treat asthma in the most severe cases.

Regardless of the medical intervention that is used, doctors note that there are additional steps people can take to keep their asthma condition under control. Using an air conditioner in the summer is key to keeping symptoms and

> "Asthma is a multifactorial disease and we need to address it from many different components, such as the environment, access to health care, public policy, health promotion and education, partnerships, surveillance, and evaluation. We need a variety of people working toward the same goal: asthma control. Nobody can do this alone."[4]
>
> —*Wanda Hernández Virella, coordinator of the Puerto Rico Asthma Project*

Keeping living spaces clean is one way to eliminate potential asthma triggers.

> By knowing how to handle their illness, people with asthma can live full, active lives.

reactions to things like pollen and pet dander under control. Vacuuming and doing a weekly clean around the house help prevent dust and mold buildup that can trigger an attack. Maintaining a healthy weight, getting plenty of exercise, and even doing breathing exercises or calming exercises such as yoga can strengthen the heart and lungs, which helps relieve asthma symptoms.

Asthma is an incurable disease. For some patients, it can be a burden at best and a life-threatening problem at worst. But living with asthma is not an impossible challenge. With the right health-care providers, a solid asthma action plan, and plenty of love and support from family and friends, asthmatics can not only live but thrive with their condition.

Essential *Facts*

Facts about Asthma

- Asthma is a disease that involves chronic inflammation of the airways.
- The major symptoms of asthma include coughing, wheezing or shortness of breath, and chest pain.
- Asthma is caused by a mix of genetic factors and environmental factors that include pollen, cold and dry weather, mold, and dust.
- More than 300 million people around the world suffer from asthma. Approximately 25 million people suffer from asthma in the United States.
- Asthma is the most common chronic health condition in children.
- There is no cure for asthma. It is possible to die from the condition, but there are many effective treatment options.

How Asthma Affects Daily Life

- Asthma affects all parts of daily life, including work, school, sports, relationships with family and friends, and stress management.
- Two types of asthma are exercise-induced bronchoconstriction and occupational asthma.
- Occupational asthma is caused by repeated exposure to allergens or toxins at work, such as sprayed chemicals, dust, latex, pet dander, and hair dye.
- Ninety percent of people who have asthma suffer from exercise-induced asthma.
- Stress and extreme emotion can cause hyperventilation, which can heighten asthma symptoms or spark an attack.

- Many people with asthma also suffer from depression if they can't participate in activities they enjoy or feel isolated from family and friends.

How Asthma Can Be Managed

- Asthma treatment involves a combination of long-term and quick-relief medications. The most commonly used long-term medications are corticosteroids. The most popular quick-relief medications are short-acting beta agonists.
- Asthma medication is delivered via a metered dose inhaler or dry powder inhaler. Combination inhalers can also be used to treat asthma.
- Surgery is rarely used to treat asthma, but bronchial thermoplasty can be done in extreme situations if recommended by a doctor.
- Biologic therapy works by targeting specific cell receptors and antibodies in the body.
- It is important to set up an asthma action plan with a doctor to keep treatment on track.

Quote

"It took me a while to accept that I was asthmatic. It took me a while to even start taking my medication properly, to do the things that the doctor was asking me to do. I just didn't want to believe that I was an asthmatic. But once I stopped living in denial, I got my asthma under control, and I realized that it is a disease that can be controlled."

—Jackie Joyner-Kersee, track-and-field star

Glossary

alleviate
To make something less severe.

antibody
A protein that the immune system uses to fight infection.

anticholinergic
A medication that blocks certain neurotransmitters, or chemical messengers, in the body to help treat diseases such as asthma.

beta agonist
A medication that relaxes the muscles surrounding the airways, allowing them to widen to make breathing easier.

bronchodilator
A medication that makes breathing easier by relaxing the muscles in the lungs and widening the airways.

cardiovascular
Relating to the heart or blood vessels.

chronic
Continuing for a long time.

corticosteroid
A drug that lowers inflammation in the body and is often used to treat asthma symptoms.

eczema
A condition that involves inflammation of the skin, including itchiness and redness.

intermittent
Happening every so often, not regularly or steadily.

mortality
A measurement of deaths in a population.

otolaryngologist
A doctor specializing in conditions of the head and neck.

pulmonary
Having to do with the lungs.

spirometry
A lung-function test that measures how much air a person breathes out and how quickly.

stethoscope
A tool doctors use to listen to a patient's heartbeat or breathing capabilities, usually consisting of a tube and two earpieces.

Additional Resources

Selected Bibliography

"Asthma." *Mayo Clinic*, 13 Sept. 2018, mayoclinic.org. Accessed 1 May 2020.

"Asthma." *National Center for Environmental Health*, 17 Mar. 2020, cdc.gov. Accessed 1 May 2020.

Carver, Melanie, Sanaz Eftekhari, and Deidre Washington. "My Life with Asthma Survey Overview." *Asthma and Allergy Foundation of America*, 2017, aafa.org. Accessed 1 May 2020.

Further Readings

Harris, Duchess, JD, PhD, with Rebecca Morris. *The Health-Care Divide*. Abdo, 2019.

Hirschmann, Kris. *Kids and Asthma*. ReferencePoint, 2019.

Human Body: A Visual Encyclopedia. DK, 2012.

Online Resources

To learn more about handling asthma, please visit **abdobooklinks.com** or scan this QR code. These links are routinely monitored and updated to provide the most current information available.

More Information

For more information on this subject, contact or visit the following organizations:

Allergy & Asthma Network
8229 Boone Blvd., Ste. 260
Vienna, VA 22182
800-878-4403
allergyasthmanetwork.org
The Allergy & Asthma Network aims to help educate patients and doctors about allergies and asthma, their causes and symptoms, possible treatment options, and the latest research developments.

American Lung Association
55 W. Wacker Dr., Ste. 1150
Chicago, IL 60601
800-586-4872
lung.org
The American Lung Association conducts research and outreach to help improve lung health and prevent lung disease.

Source Notes

CHAPTER 1. A HURDLE TO A DREAM

1. "Turning Discovery into Health—Asthma." *Medline Plus*, 2011, magazine.medlineplus.gov. Accessed 8 July 2020.
2. "Asthma." *World Health Organization*, 15 May 2020, who.int. Accessed 8 May 2020.
3. "Asthma." *Centers for Disease Control and Prevention*, 24 Mar. 2020, cdc.gov. Accessed 8 May 2020.
4. "'There's No Reason You Shouldn't Be the Best." *Asthma UK*, July 2016, asthma.org.uk. Accessed 8 July 2020.
5. "Asthma Facts and Figures." *Asthma and Allergy Foundation of America*, June 2019, aafa.org. Accessed 8 July 2020.
6. Joshua Davidson. "The Effect of Asthma on Long-Term Health." *Verywell Health*, 4 Dec. 2019, verywellhealth.com. Accessed 8 July 2020.

CHAPTER 2. SYMPTOMS AND CAUSES

1. Pat Bass. "What Is Asthma?" *Verywell Health*, 6 Dec. 2019, verywellhealth.com. Accessed 8 July 2020.
2. Elana Pearl Ben-Joseph. "Smoking and Asthma." *KidsHealth*, June 2016, kidshealth.org. Accessed 8 July 2020.
3. "Asthma." *Centers for Disease Control and Prevention*, 23 Mar. 2020, cdc.gov. Accessed 8 July 2020.
4. Serena Gordon. "More Studies Link Vaping to Asthma, COPD." *WebMD*, 14 Jan. 2020, webmd.com. Accessed 8 July 2020.
5. Pat Bass. "Causes and Risk Factors of Asthma." *Verywell Health*, 31 Oct. 2019, verywellhealth.com. Accessed 8 July 2020.
6. Vann R. Newkirk II. "How to Beat Asthma." *Atlantic*, 5 July 2017, theatlantic.com. Accessed 8 July 2020.
7. Diana Rodriguez. "What We Know about the Link between Obesity and Asthma." *Everyday Health*, 16 Oct. 2019, everydayhealth.com. Accessed 8 July 2020.
8. Jenna Fletcher. "Does Asthma Run in the Family?" *Medical News Today*, 14 Feb. 2019, medicalnewstoday.com. Accessed 8 July 2020.

CHAPTER 3. GETTING A DIAGNOSIS

1. "How Do You Feel about Your Asthma?" *Asthma UK*, Jan. 2019, asthma.org.uk. Accessed 8 July 2020.
2. Bruce Jancin. "When and How to Suspect Asthma Misdiagnosis." *Pulmonary Health Hub*, 7 May 2018, mdedge.com. Accessed 8 July 2020.
3. "Asthma." *National Heart, Lung, and Blood Institute*, 21 May 2020, nhlbi.nih.gov. Accessed 8 July 2020.
4. "What Are the Symptoms of Asthma?" *Allergy & Asthma Network*, 2020, allergyasthmanetwork.org. Accessed 8 July 2020.
5. "Greg Hebrank – Severe Asthma." *UPMC Children's Hospital of Pittsburgh*, 2020, chp.edu. Accessed 8 July 2020.
6. "Greg Hebrank – Severe Asthma."
7. "Greg Hebrank – Severe Asthma."
8. "Greg Hebrank – Severe Asthma."

CHAPTER 4. DISEASE DEMOGRAPHICS

1. "Centres." *Global Asthma Network*, n.d., globalasthmanetwork.org. Accessed 8 July 2020.
2. "The Global Asthma Report 2018." *Global Asthma Network*, n.d., globalasthmareport.org. Accessed 8 July 2020.
3. "Asthma Facts and Figures." *Asthma and Allergy Foundation of America*, June 2019, aafa.org. Accessed 8 July 2020.
4. "Asthma Facts and Figures."
5. "What Is Asthma?" *Global Asthma Network*, n.d., globalasthmareport.org. Accessed 8 July 2020.
6. "Asthma Facts and Figures."
7. "Asthma Facts and Figures."
8. "Asthma." *Centers for Disease Control and Prevention*, 24 Mar. 2020, cdc.gov. Accessed 8 May 2020.
9. "Most Recent National Asthma Data." *CDC*, 24 Mar. 2020, cdc.gov. Accessed 22 July 2020.
10. Allison Inserro. "CDC Study Puts Economic Burden of Asthma at More than $80 Billion Per Year." *AJMC*, 12 Jan. 2018, ajmc.com. Accessed 8 July 2020.
11. Vann R. Newkirk II. "How to Beat Asthma." *Atlantic*, 5 July 2017, theatlantic.com. Accessed 8 July 2020.

Source Notes Continued

CHAPTER 5. THE HISTORY OF ASTHMA

1. Adam Felman. "A Brief History of Asthma." *Medical News Today*, 2 Nov. 2018, medicalnewstoday.com. Accessed 8 July 2020.

2. Marianna Karamanou and G. Androutsos. "Aretaeus of Cappadocia and the First Clinical Description of Asthma." *American Thoracic Society Journals*, 2011, atsjournals.org. Accessed 8 July 2020.

3. Karamanou and Androutsos, "Aretaeus of Cappadocia and the First Clinical Description of Asthma."

4. "Chapter 55—Remedies for Liver Complaints and for Asthma." *Pliny the Elder*, perseus.tufts.edu. Accessed 8 July 2020.

5. Alex Sakula. "Henry Hyde Salter (1823–71): A Biographical Sketch." *Thorax*, 1985, thorax.bmj.com. Accessed 8 July 2020.

6. Vann R. Newkirk II. "How to Beat Asthma." *Atlantic*, 5 July 2017, theatlantic.com. Accessed 8 July 2020.

CHAPTER 6. ASTHMA AND PHYSICAL HEALTH

1. "Reading Teenager Winning His Battle with Asthma." *Reading Hospital*, 29 May 2019, reading.towerhealth.org. Accessed 8 July 2020.

2. "Reading Teenager Winning His Battle with Asthma."

3. "Reading Teenager Winning His Battle with Asthma."

4. "Reading Teenager Winning His Battle with Asthma."

5. "Medical History." *BreathinStephen*, 10 June 2020, breathinstephen.com. Accessed 8 July 2020.

6. "Sleep? What the Heck Is That?" *BreathinStephen*, 21 Feb. 2020, breathinstephen.com. Accessed 8 July 2020.

7. "Reading Teenager Winning His Battle with Asthma."

8. "Exercise-Induced Asthma." *Mayo Clinic*, 16 Oct. 2018, mayoclinic.org. Accessed 8 July 2020.

9. Jonathan Parsons. "Out of Shape, or Exercise-Induced Asthma?" *Ohio State University Wexner Medical Center*, 6 Nov. 2017, wexnermedical.osu.edu. Accessed 8 July 2020.

10. Pamela Babcock. "10 Risky Jobs for Your Lungs." *WebMD*, 2019, webmd.com. Accessed 8 July 2020.

11. Babcock, "10 Risky Jobs for Your Lungs."

CHAPTER 7. ASTHMA AND MENTAL HEALTH

1. "Living with Asthma: Alex's Story." *British Lung Foundation*, 2 May 2017, blf.org.uk. Accessed 8 July 2020.
2. "Living with Asthma: Alex's Story."
3. "Living with Asthma: Alex's Story."
4. "The Anxiety of Asthma: Emotions Can Trigger Attack." *WebMD*, 7 Apr. 2001, webmd.com. Accessed 8 July 2020.
5. Karon Warren. "Severe Asthma: 8 Things Doctors Want You to Know." *Healthgrades*, 21 Mar. 2018, healthgrades.com. Accessed 8 July 2020.
6. "The Anxiety of Asthma: Emotions Can Trigger Attack."
7. "Families with Healthy Kids – Not Fair!!" *My Life as an Asthma Mom*, 23 Jan. 2020, asthmamomlife.blogspot.com. Accessed 8 July 2020.
8. "My Life with Asthma." *Asthma and Allergy Foundation of America*, n.d., aafa.org. Accessed 8 July 2020.
9. "My Life with Asthma."
10. Carol Sorgen. "Coping with Asthma Stress as a Family." *Verywell Health*, 13 Dec. 2019, verywellhealth.com. Accessed 8 July 2020.
11. "My Life with Asthma."
12. Sorgen, "Coping With Asthma Stress as a Family."
13. Okan Elidemir. "Managing Asthma." *KidsHealth*, Feb. 2019, kidshealth.org. Accessed 8 July 2020.

CHAPTER 8. TREATMENT AND BEYOND

1. Karon Warren. "Severe Asthma: 8 Things Doctors Want You to Know." *Healthgrades*, 21 Mar. 2018, healthgrades.com. Accessed 8 July 2020.
2. Warren, "Severe Asthma: 8 Things Doctors Want You to Know."
3. "Severe Asthma and Allergies: Mena's Story." *Children's Hospital of Philadelphia*, 22 May 2019, chop.edu. Accessed 8 July 2020.
4. "Breathing Easier in Puerto Rico." *Centers for Disease Control and Prevention*, n.d., cdc.gov. Accessed 8 July 2020.

Index

allergies, 9, 30, 37, 71, 80, 91, 92
allergists, 7–8, 29
allergy medications, 92
American Academy of Allergy Asthma & Immunology, 69
American Lung Association, 27
antibodies, 95–96
anticholinergics, 93
anxiety, 31, 75, 78, 79, 80
apps, 60–61
Ardiles, Thomas, 87
Aretaeus of Cappadocia, 53, 54
aspirin, 25
asthma action plan, 10, 87–88, 99
Asthma and Allergy Foundation of America, 24, 81, 83, 85
asthma categories, 34–35

Ben-Joseph, Elana Pearl, 22
beta-blockers, 25
biologic therapy, 95–96
bronchial thermoplasty, 91
bronchodilators, 12, 58

cancer, 23, 73
caregivers, 48, 61, 82, 84–85
Centers for Disease Control and Prevention (CDC), 9, 13, 23, 42, 44, 69
chronic obstructive pulmonary disease (COPD), 30, 31, 73
corticosteroids, 58, 64, 89, 91, 92, 93
COVID-19, 20

Davidson, Joshua, 15
demographics, 41–45
diagnosis, 8–9, 21, 24, 29–39, 59

Ebers papyrus, 52
eczema, 9
Elidemir, Okan, 85
environmental causes, 21–25, 46, 48, 52, 69, 73
exercise-induced asthma, 23–24, 66–69

Felix, Allyson, 6
Food and Drug Administration (FDA), 58
forced expiratory volume (FEV), 9
forced vital capacity (FVC), 9

gastroesophageal reflux disease (GERD), 26, 31
genetics, 21, 25–27, 57
Global Asthma Network (GAN), 41

Harber, Philip, 72–73
health care access, 45–49
Healthy Kids Express, 48
healthy lifestyle, 10–11, 99
high altitudes, 24–25
Hippocrates, 52, 79
histamines, 80
hyperventilation, 80

ibuprofen, 25
immune system, 58, 77, 80, 92
inflammation, 12, 23, 31, 51, 58, 87, 91, 93, 95, 96
inhalers, 49, 52, 57, 60, 88, 89
  combination inhalers, 12
  quick-relief inhalers, 10, 29, 66, 92–93

Joyner-Kersee, Jackie, 5–6, 7

language barriers, 46–47
leukotriene modifiers, 90–91
long-acting beta agonists, 91

Maimonides, 54
Mayo Clinic, 30, 34, 96
methacholine challenge, 32
mortality rates, 44–45
Mudge, John, 57

naproxen sodium, 25
National Institutes of Health (NIH), 78
nebulizers, 57, 89, 93
nitric oxide test, 32
nocturnal asthma, 35

obesity, 26–27
occupational asthma, 69–73
Osler, William, 56–57

peak flow meter, 31–32, 34, 37, 59, 61, 88
pet dander, 21, 99
Pliny the Elder, 53, 54
pollen, 21, 37, 53, 66, 69, 91, 92, 99
prevalence, 13, 42
Puerto Rico, 46, 96

Radcliffe, Paula, 6, 13
relationships, 14, 25, 78, 81–85
respiratory system, 17–18

Salter, Henry Hyde, 54–55
school, 14, 48, 82
short-acting beta agonists, 93
sleep, 19, 35, 38, 65, 66, 73, 80
smoking, 22–23, 24
spirometers, 9, 31, 33, 34, 54, 60–61
stress-induced asthma, 25, 57, 78–81
symptoms
  chest pain, 19, 31, 52, 64, 80
  congestion, 9, 80
  coughing, 19, 20, 23, 25, 35, 64, 80
  shortness of breath, 19, 20, 23, 29, 35, 64
  wheezing, 9, 19, 20, 23, 25, 29, 35, 51, 64, 67, 80

theophylline, 91–92

vaping, 23, 26

Weinstein, Andrew G., 79
work, 14, 22, 69–73
World Asthma Day, 76, 78
World Health Organization (WHO), 41, 51
Wright, Martin, 59

yoga, 68, 99
young children, 21, 34

About the Author

Alexis Burling

Alexis Burling has written dozens of articles and books for young readers on a variety of topics, including current events, nutrition and fitness, careers and money management, relationships, and cooking. She is also a book critic with reviews of both adult and young adult books, author interviews, and other industry-related articles published in the *New York Times*, *Washington Post*, *San Francisco Chronicle*, and more. Burling lives in Portland, Oregon, with her husband.

About the Consultant
Jennifer Shih, MD

Jennifer Shih, MD, is a board-certified physician and assistant professor in the department of medicine and pediatrics at Emory University, where she serves as medical director of the Allergy/Immunology section. She practices allergy, asthma, and immunology at Children's Healthcare of Atlanta and adult Emory Clinics. She received her doctorate of medicine from Louisiana State University Medical School in New Orleans as one of ten students in the accelerated medical school program. She subsequently completed residency and allergy/immunology fellowship training at Emory University. She has presented at multiple national meetings with research interests including asthma, food allergy, and telemedicine. Dr. Shih has lived in Atlanta for several years with her husband, twin daughters, and dog. She enjoys spending time with her family, traveling, and planning for her nonprofit, which assists transplant patients.